Destiny's
REVELATIONS

Look for these and other books about Linelle Destiny in the Linelle Destiny Series:

Visit www.thesecretsistersclub.com

Linelle Destiny Series

Destiny's
REVELATIONS

Dr. Alicia Holland
Illustrations by Anoop PC

This book may be ordered through booksellers or by contacting:

iGlobal Educational Services, LLC
PO Box 94224
Phoenix, Arizona 85070
www.iglobaleducation.com
512-761-5898

Because of the dynamic nature of the Internet, any web addresses or links contained in this book may have changed since publication and may no longer be valid. The views expressed in this work are solely those of the author and do not necessarily reflect the views of the publisher, and the publisher hereby disclaims any responsibility for them.

This is a work of fiction. Names, characters, businesses, places, events, and incidents are either the products of the author's imagination or used in a fictitious manner. Any resemblance to actual persons, living or dead, or actual events is purely coincidental.

Linelle Destiny Series: **Destiny's Revelations**

Copyright © 2018 Alicia Holland, EdD. All Rights Reserved.

ISBN-13: 978-1-944346-19-5

Acknowledgements

I want to first honor God for placing in my heart to share my story with others. It was He whom brought Karen and I together to manifest this project. I am so grateful for Karen Hendry as she took my notes and helped write this fictitious book. There are truly no words to express my gratitude as you are truly a blessing.

I also want to thank Surendra Gupta for his creativity in formatting and Anoop PC for his creativity in bringing life to the designs and illustrations in this book series. Both of you are amazing!

Dedication

I dedicate this book series to my beautiful and talented daughters, Georgia and Amaiya Johnson. Remember, you are valued, loved, and competent. You are worthy!

Part 1:
Back-to-School Bash

Chapter 1
Planning

S ummer is nearly over, and once again Destiny is getting ready for the start of the new school year. Sitting in the quiet of her office at the tutoring center, Destiny is planning the big Back-to-School Bash they are hosting for the tutoring students. The bash will be a fun party and a great way to kick off the new school and tutoring year.

Destiny can hear Shelley puttering around out in the main room of the center. She is going through the various materials they have, taking inventory, and preparing work for returning students who have been away for the summer. Destiny encourages her students to keep at their studies through the summer, but many of them have travel plans and miss much of it.

There have also been a lot of new student signing up. Destiny has had Reginae come in a few days this past week to help register new students and take care of the paperwork involved. Yes, the beginning of the school year is definitely a busy time.

Destiny is trying to think of a fun activity they can include at the bash, which is happening in three days. She just needs one more thing to fill in about an hour of the time. Maybe they could hold a race in the park across the street.

Destiny leaves her office to look for Shelley, who she finds sorting through the grades one to three tutoring material. Shelley looks up from what she is doing. "Well, look who decided to emerge from her office and see the light of day."

"Only for a moment," replies Destiny. "What do you think of holding a race as part of the Back-to-School Bash? After all, we have the school's track at our disposal."

"That's a great idea. We could set up some games for the younger kids and have the older kids race. Prizes?"

"Absolutely!"

"Since we have the track we could hold a 5K race," says Shelley.

"That sounds great."

"Well," says Shelley with a grin on her face. "I guess we have more work to do now."

Destiny sighs. "I guess we do. I'd better get back to it."

Destiny hasn't even been in her office for five minutes when Shelley pops her head in. "Someone here to see you. Says her name is Ethel?"

"Really? That's great. She is one of my colleagues from the school. Another math teacher." Destiny stands up from her desk. "Come and meet her. She's wonderful."

Destiny walks out to find Ethel browsing through some of the teaching material on one of the shelves. "Ethel!" she says as she goes over and gives her colleague a hug. "How are you? How has your summer been?"

"Can't complain, Destiny, other than to say it's been too short. Honestly, I swear it gets shorter and shorter every year. But only a few more to go until retirement. It's the idea of that and the kids keep me going."

"You could never retire," says Destiny.

"Oh, yes I could. When the time comes, I'll miss my colleagues and I'll miss the kids terribly, but I will *not* miss the bureaucracy."

"Fair enough," says Destiny. "Ethel, I'd like you to meet Shelley. She is my assistant manager here at the center."

Ethel reaches out and shakes Shelley's hand. "Pleased to meet you, Shelley. I am so glad Destiny has made good use of you around here. Last year she nearly killed herself trying to do everything."

"That is the truth," says Shelley. "Pleased to meet you, too. Now, if you will please excuse me, I have a lot to do."

Shelley retreats to the table she was sitting at and Ethel says, "So, are you going to give me a tour of the incredible tutoring center, or what?"

They walk through the center and Destiny shows Ethel the various stations that are set up for the different grades. By the time they reach Destiny's office door, Ethel is saying, "Destiny, this center is amazing! I can't believe the resources you have here. And you have developed the curriculum yourself?"

Destiny nods, smiling with pride at the praise from Ethel. Ethel has been teaching for many years. Destiny really respects her. If she is impressed, then Destiny knows she has done a good job.

"Oh, and I haven't even asked how your summer was. How rude of me. Did you get at least a little time off to relax?"

Ethel sees the sheepish look on Destiny's face. "Uh huh," she says. "I figured as much. You look tired. Not quite as tired as last spring, but still."

"I'm feeling good, though," says Destiny. "Busy, but good. I'll be here all evening getting things ready for our Back-to-School Bash this weekend."

"Well, you need to take a break for some dinner. Why don't you join me?"

Destiny hesitates. She was just going to have a working dinner while she tried to get some things done.

"Come on, now. It will do you good to get out of here for a while. And I assume Calix isn't expecting you home, so you really don't have any excuse. Besides, I need the company."

"Oh, okay," says Destiny. "Just let me get my purse and we'll go. The diner down the street okay?"

"Sure is. And let's invite Shelley. She could probably use a break, too."

A couple of minutes later, Destiny and Ethel are heading out the door. Despite their best efforts, Shelley could not be persuaded to go with them. She had a nice meal she had brought from home and was in the middle of organizing one of the stations.

Once outside, Destiny takes a deep breath of fresh air. Yes, Ethel was right. Getting out of the center for a while is a good idea.

Once at the diner and seated, Destiny and Ethel order. Destiny is starving and really feels like having a great big burger, so she orders one that is loaded. But for some reason, she can't imagine eating French fries with it. The thought of eating them turns her off so she orders onion rings instead.

"You sure you can eat that big old burger?" asks Ethel.

"Oh yeah. I'm famished."

Ethel stares at Destiny, one eyebrow raised. Then she says, "So, are you looking forward to the school year starting?"

"Yes and no," says Destiny. "I'm looking forward to working with the kids, but I am still wary of Daniella."

Principal Daniella Brandfather had given Destiny such a hard time for most of the last school year, she isn't sure what to expect in the coming year.

"I understand. She eased up a little near the end, though, didn't she?"

"A little," says Destiny as a giant burger is placed in front of her. Ethel has a bowl of soup.

"Now, how are you going to eat that?" asks Ethel.

"One bite at a time," Destiny replies. Taking a bite of an onion ring.

"I don't know," says Destiny, after she finishes chewing. "I've been at this school for two years now and I feel as if I don't know how to manage there. I feel like I am still an outsider in so many ways."

"Dear, I understand. But you aren't. Everyone loves you and appreciates your contributions."

"Everyone, but Daniella," says Destiny.

"I think she does, too, in her own way. But there are certainly some unwritten rules in that school. If you follow them, you'll do fine."

"Really? And they are?"

"Well, the first is 'do as I say, and not as I do.'"

"Well, that would be Daniella's rule for sure."

Ethel nods. "And if you want favoritism, there are two things to do. One is get in on the gossip."

"Not me," says Destiny. "I refuse to speak at the expense of others."

"And spend time with Daniella outside of work."

"She can't even stand me at work! How on earth would I ever be able to get together with her outside of work?"

"I don't know, dear. Maybe invite her to your big bash you're having for the center."

"I suppose I could," says Destiny thoughtfully. "But I seriously doubt she'd come, even if it is being held at the school."

"No harm in asking."

"That's true enough."

They finish their meals as they talk about the coming school year. Then they say their goodbyes and Destiny heads back to the center. Yes, maybe she should invite Principal Brandfather to the Back-to-School Bash. Even if she doesn't come, at least Destiny will have made the effort.

Destiny decides she will give Principal Brandfather a call when she gets back to the center. The worst she can say is "no." Then Destiny realizes she would actually be pleased if Principal Brandfather did come. Destiny giggles a little. She sure is a dreamer.

Chapter 2

Big Bash

Destiny stands on her tip toes to get a better view. She has to shade her eyes, despite the fact that the day started off with a cloudy sky. There are so many people that have come for the Back-to-School Bash and she is thrilled beyond belief. It's the first time she has ever held such an event.

But right now, Destiny isn't counting heads. She is looking for someone. When she called Principal Brandfather, there was no answer so she left a message. She also sent Principal Brandfather an email. She didn't get a reply to either.

Destiny isn't surprised. Not really. But for some reason, she was holding out hope the Principal Brandfather would show up. It would have been so nice for her to come and see what Destiny is doing with the kids in her center. Plus, her office is just inside the building.

Then again, the only reason Destiny is even holding the event at the school was because she has to rent the facility through the school board. If Principal Brandfather had any say in it, they wouldn't be here.

Someone touches Destiny's arm and she jumps. Shelley has come up behind her.

"Sorry, didn't mean to startle you," says Shelley.

"Oh, that's okay," Destiny replies.

"Looks like Georgia is having fun."

Destiny looks in the direction Shelley is pointing and sees Georgia reaching for the bubbles that float over her head. She certainly has plenty of company with many of Destiny's students paying loads of attention to her. Destiny sees Calix sitting at a picnic table chatting with one of the parents.

"Were you looking for someone?" asks Shelley.

"Yeah, sort of. Well, I left a message and invited my principal to come today."

"She's coming?" Destiny can hear the astonishment in Shelley's voice. Destiny has told her all about Principal Brandfather and the way she has behaved over the past year.

"No, I don't think so. I never got a response from her. I was really just hoping, I guess."

"Well, you don't need her here raining on your parade. The turnout is amazing. There are so many families here. And I think it is time we got this event underway."

Destiny nods and steps up onto the seat of a nearby bench. "Excuse me," she says into the microphone they set up. "Excuse me, everyone."

Destiny waits a few moments as people begin to quiet down and turn to look her way.

"I just wanted to thank you all for coming and welcome you here on this beautiful day."

Every cheers and claps.

When the noise dies down, Destiny continues. "We have lots of activities planned for you today. To my right is a games area we have set up for the younger students." Destiny gestures with her hand as she speaks. "And to my left is a food station, so if anyone is hungry, that's the place to be."

More cheering.

"Finally, we have the set up for the big 5K race we are holding for the older students."

Destiny can hear the cheers coming from the students. She smiles as she continues. "The race will begin in 15 minutes and the starting line is marked on the track. So, don't eat too much food, yet."

Laughter.

"Please, students participating in the race, make your way to the track. And everyone, have a great time and come say hello to me and to my fantastic staff who have helped make this event become a reality."

Huge applause erupts as Destiny steps down from the bench. It's too bad Principal Brandfather didn't come today, but it's her loss because this is going to be a super fun day.

Destiny makes her way to the start line of the race, chatting with parents and student along the way. Calix, Shelley, and some of Destiny's other staff join her.

There are close to a dozen students gathered at the start line. Destiny is happy to see them there and more keep trickling in.

By the time the race is due to start, there are over 20 students ready to race. Destiny speaks to them, "Welcome to our 5K race everyone! I am proud of you for joining in. You will be running around the track 12 and a half times! It's a good thing you all have a fresh breeze to cool you down as you run!"

Everyone laughs, but they are also nodding their heads. The breezed is a relief.

"The finish line will be set up as the race gets close to the finish."

Everyone nods and cheers.

"I have asked my wonderful husband, Calix, to start the race. He has a big booming voice. Calix?"

"Thanks, Destiny. Hi everyone! Welcome to the 5K race. Will everyone please line up at the start line?"

The students do as he asks. It takes a moment for them to get organized.

Then Calix shouts, "On your marks." The students look down the long stretch of track that lies in front of them. Some crouch like they are a runner at the Olympics.

"Get set! Go!"

And away they go. The cheering starts immediately and it is an absolutely thrilling race. About 25 minutes after the start of the race, Destiny and Shelley take the long red ribbon over to the finish line. Destiny's staff have been keeping track of the laps the runners have made. Some are slower and some are faster, but the winner is clear.

One of Destiny's students from last school year, Devon, who still studies at the center is way ahead of the pack. When he is heading around the bend to run the last stretch, Destiny and Shelley stretch the ribbon across the track.

As Devon runs through the ribbon a huge cheer goes up. Everyone is thrilled to see the winner of the race. Devon is fist pumping and jumping up and down he is so happy. At the same time, he is panting with the exertion of the run.

His parents congratulate him and then everyone else is crowding around. The next runner comes in a couple of minutes after Devon and the other runners make their way through their final laps. Fifteen minutes later, the race is over.

Destiny walks up to Devon and shakes his sweaty hand. "Great job, Devon!"

The second and third place winners are also nearby. Destiny brings them all to the bench where the microphone is located and steps up onto the bench once again, microphone in hand.

"Can I have everyone's attention?"

After a moment, the crowd settles down.

"I want to announce the winners of the 5K race. In first place, winning two months of free tuition at the center, is Devon!"

Everyone cheers and Destiny can hear a group of kids whooping at the tops of their lungs. Clearly, Devon's friends.

"In second place, Whitney, and in third place, Gerry. They each win one free month's tuition."

More cheering.

"Now," says Destiny, shouting over the crowd, despite having a microphone. "Enjoy the rest of the bash!"

The day turns out to be a bigger success than Destiny anticipated. Everyone had such a great time. Georgia sleeps the entire way home. Destiny looks back at her and says, "I wish I could fall asleep like that. I'm exhausted."

"It was a busy day," replies Calix.

"It was a fabulous day," says Destiny through a yawn.

A few minutes later, they pull into their driveway. The bump of the small curb entering the driveway nudges Destiny awake and she realizes she nodded off. She looks at Calix and he is smiling at her.

"Looks like you *can* fall asleep like she does."

They take Georgia inside and Calix unloads the cooler and other things from the truck.

Inside, Destiny takes Georgia out of her car seat. Georgia is wide awake now, and giggles at Destiny. Destiny sighs. She doesn't have the energy for Georgia right now.

Calix comes in and says, "I can take her if you want to rest."

"That would be super."

Destiny leaves everything to Calix and heads into the bedroom to get changed into her PJs. Stifling another yawn, she brushes her teeth, washes her face, and gets a glass of water. Then she settles in bed with a paper she is reading. She tries to read, but she just keeps reading the same line over and over again. Her eyes are getting heavy. Then she is asleep.

Chapter 3

Unexpected News

Five days later, Destiny is sitting in the examination room at her doctor's office. She is reading the heart disease information poster on the wall for the fifth time. She has read all the other posters multiple times, too.

Destiny hates waiting for the doctor. It always seems to take so long and there are so many other things she could be doing right now. And she has already been through this once this week. She came in three days ago to find out why she has been so tired.

Dr. Henderson had checked her over and didn't find anything during the examination. He also ordered blood work and she had gone right to the lab just to get it over with. Maybe her iron levels are low. Destiny knows she hasn't been eating properly.

A light knock comes at the door. "Come in," says Destiny.

"Hi, Destiny," says Dr. Henderson cheerfully as he slides into the room. "How are you feeling today?"

"Fine, but still tired."

"Yes, well, I don't doubt it."

"You figured out what's wrong with me?"

Dr. Henderson laughs a high-pitched kind of squeak for a man. "Destiny, there isn't a thing wrong with you."

"I don't understand," says Destiny. "Then why am I always so tired?"

"You're going to have a baby!"

Destiny doesn't say anything at first. She processes what Dr. Henderson just said. A baby. A baby!

"I'm pregnant?"

"Yes, my darlin', you sure are, Dr. Henderson drawls in his thick Texan accent. "About 10 weeks along, I'd wager."

Destiny doesn't know what to say, but it all makes sense. Now that she thinks about it, this is exactly how she felt with Georgia. All the signs were there and she was too busy to see them.

"You weren't plannin' this one, were you?" asks Dr. Henderson.

"Ah, no. No, we weren't. It's really quite a surprise," answers Destiny.

"Well, I can't think of a better surprise," Dr. Henderson says. "Can you?"

"No, I suppose not," says Destiny.

"Now, I want you to come back and see me in two weeks for a checkup. You hear?"

"Yes, okay."

"Alright, we'll be seeing you soon." And then Dr. Henderson is gone and Destiny is still sitting there all alone. She hears a child cry out from a room down the hall and it snaps her out of her stupor.

She stands up, walks out of the room, and makes an appointment at reception before heading outside. The sun feels warm on her face and she stands there for a moment, with her eyes closed, face raised to the warmth.

She looks calm on the outside, but her mind is full of thoughts, flying around like bats in a cave. She's so busy. She can barely handle Georgia and everything she's doing. How will she be able to take care of a new baby on top of it all?

Then she gives herself a mental shake. She has Calix and they are a team. Together they will figure this out because together they can handle everything. Besides, they have plenty of other people in their lives to help out. And it will be nice for Georgia to have a little brother or sister to play with.

That thought makes Destiny smile as she walks to her truck and gets in. Yes, she thinks, everything is going to be just fine.

As Georgia plays in the dining room, Destiny sets the table and gets dinner out of the oven. She glances at the clock on the microwave—5:32. Calix should be home soon. For some reason, Destiny feels nervous butterflies fluttering around in her stomach.

Then she hears the front door open and the familiar sound of his boots in the hallway. A couple of minutes later, Calix is in the dining room, whisking Georgia into his arms. She giggles as he twirls her around. Daddy's girl.

"Hey," he says to Destiny.

"Hey."

"Dinner smells great. I'm starving."

"Well, then," says Destiny, "let's eat."

Calix puts Georgia in her high chair and they each dish out the casserole Destiny made. The first couple of minutes is silent as Calix eats.

"So," says Destiny, "how was your day?"

"It was okay. Still having issues with Dwayne, but you know how he is."

Destiny nods.

"Well, I had an interesting day," she says.

"Oh yeah? How so?"

"Well, I went to the doctor."

"Right, he had some test results for you. Everything okay?"

Destiny nods again. There is a grin plastered on her face. She knows it, but she just can't help it.

"I've been so tired because I'm pregnant, Calix."

Calix stops chewing and just stares at her.

"Well?" says Destiny. "You're awfully quiet."

"Sorry," Calix responds finally. "It's… I just wasn't expecting…"

"I know. Neither was I," says Destiny. "At first, I was terrified, but now I'm actually elated. Georgia will be a big sister and we will have someone else in our home to love."

Calix says, "I just hope it won't be too much. I mean, you have so much on your plate right now. We're both stretched pretty thin."

"I know, but we'll manage somehow. We always do. We have lots of people to help. We have Madeline, who would love another little one to take care of for us. And everyone at the center will help out, too."

"You're right," Calix says as he stands up and puts his plate in the dishwasher. "We do have plenty of help."

Destiny stands up and looks up at him. "So, you're okay with this? You're happy."

He puts his hands on her shoulders and kisses her on the forehead. "Of course, I am," he says with a smile. "Now, I think it's my turn to give Georgia a bath. I'll do that while you clean up."

He hugs Destiny and gets Georgia and a couple of minutes later, she can hear the faint sound of the water running through the pipes to the bathtub.

As she clears the table, Destiny feels relieved that Calix is happy about the baby. But she has a nagging feeling that something is off. He said all the right things and seemed fine, if a little surprised. But there was something missing in his eyes, a certain...

Destiny just can't put her finger on it. But as she puts the leftovers in the fridge she thinks it is probably just the timing. After all, it's far from ideal. That's probably all it is. Besides, she's had all afternoon to get used to the idea. He'll get there, too.

Destiny goes into the living room after cleaning up the kitchen and decides to call Katie. She wants to share her good news with someone other than Calix. Besides, she hasn't spoken to Katie all summer, even though she has tried to call Katie several times.

Destiny knows why. Ever since she told Katie about Fred and his behavior, Katie has been avoiding her and not returning her calls. But Destiny hasn't tried in a couple of weeks. Hopefully, Katie has come around by now. After all, Destiny might not like Fred, but she sure does miss her friend. And she could use that friend right now.

She dials Katie's number and the phone rings once before it stops. Hmm, thinks Destiny as she hangs up. Katie must be on the phone right now. At least, that's what Destiny tells herself. She decides she'll try Katie again another time.

Besides, she has work to do on her thesis and she had better get it done while she has the energy left to do it. So, as Georgia's sweet giggles carry down from upstairs, Destiny sits down at her desk and digs into her work.

Part 2:
Back to School

Chapter 4

First Day

Pulling her chair in, Destiny settles in at her desk. She pulls out her class list and goes through the names. She is thrilled to see she recognizes some of the names from the Back-to-Bash. It's nice knowing she will start the school year knowing some of the students ahead of time.

As Destiny is pulling out her lesson plan, Ethel's voice rings out in the empty classroom. "Good morning, Destiny! It's the start of another beautiful year."

Destiny looks up and smiles as Ethel strides into the room. "Yes, it is," Destiny replies.

"It's going to be a good year. I can feel it already. How does your class look?"

Destiny glances down at her class list. "It looks great. I get to work with some of the students at the center and quite a few of them were at the Back-to-School Bash. It's nice to start the year with some familiarity, you know?"

"I sure do. And how is your research going?"

"Pretty good," says Destiny. "I need to start collecting data now. I have all I need right here in my classroom, but I am almost certain I'll run into a roadblock, if you know what I mean."

Ethel nods. "You don't think Daniella will actually refuse you, will she?"

"I wouldn't put anything past her."

"Hmm," says Ethel. "Well, I hope not. Honestly, egos shouldn't get in the way of progress and helping the children."

"Try telling that to her."

"Anything else new?" asks Ethel.

Destiny smiles, "Yes, actually."

"You're not! When are you due?"

"How did you know?"

"I'd know that look anywhere, honey."

"Early March," says Destiny. "Just one more reason for her to hate me."

"Oh, you never mind that old bat. This is so exciting! Although, you are a glutton for punishment. I mean, I don't know how you find the time do manage everything now."

"Well, this isn't something we planned, but we'll make it work."

"You know I'm always around to help out."

"Thanks, Ethel."

"Okay, I'm off to get ready. They'll start arriving soon."

Destiny loves how giddy Ethel always is on the first day of school. It's almost infectious, because as the first of Destiny's students begin to filter into the room, she can't help but feel a surge of excitement.

✧ ✧ ✧

The last of Destiny's students claims their seat as the bell rings and Destiny introduces herself. "Good morning! I bet you are all happy to be back."

She hears many groans and she smiles even more. "Some of you might already know me, but for those who don't, I'm Ms. Sycamores and I will be your homeroom and math teacher this year. We are going to begin by taking attendance and perhaps today each of you can stand up when I say your name so everyone can put a face to that name."

Destiny goes through the names and everyone on her list is present. As Destiny goes to her desk and puts down the class list, one student near the back of the class speaks up.

"Excuse me, Ms. Sycamores?"

"Yes, Jasmine." Destiny knows this girl from the center.

"I just wanted to thank you for the Back-to-School Bash. It was so much fun."

"It was," says Henry from closer to the front of the class.

"Thank you very much," says Destiny. "How many of you were there?" Nine students raise their hand. "I'm glad you had such a good time."

The other students look a bit confused so Destiny explains what the Back-to-School Bash is. "And now," says Destiny, "let's get to work."

A new round of groans as the students take out their books. Destiny can tell it's going to be a fun year.

Destiny looks into her mailbox, but it's empty. It's a final check before she heads home for the day. Just then, Principal Brandfather walks into the office. Destiny hasn't seen her all day. She follows Principal Brandfather into her office.

"Excuse me, Daniella," says Destiny. "Can I speak with you for a moment?"

Destiny can see the impatience on Principal Brandfather's face. She doesn't even try to hide it. "Yes, I suppose."

"How was your summer?" asks Destiny to break through the wall of ice between them.

"It was fine, thanks. What do you need?"

Wow, thinks Destiny. This is cold even for Daniella. "As you know, I'm working on my PhD and I am ready to start collecting data. Can I ask you to sign this form so I can use the students in my class?"

"Absolutely not."

"I assure you, everything will be kept completely anonymous. No student will ever be identified by name."

"Destiny, whatever you do outside of your work time is of your own concern. I can't do anything about that, but I will not allow it to come through these doors and affect my students. It is inappropriate for you to even ask such a thing."

"With all due respect, Daniella, it is entirely common for PhD students to collect class data. That's how we learn about the students and make things better for them. It's in their best interests. And unlike many PhD students, I am fortunate enough to have a class of my own. I really don't see the problem."

"No, I don't suppose you do," says Principal Brandfather. "Still, I won't allow it in my school."

Principal Brandfather looks down at the papers on her desk and begins to work. Clearly, Destiny has been dismissed. And this is definitely *not* the time to tell Principal Brandfather she's pregnant.

Destiny leaves the school feeling more than a little discouraged. What is her problem, anyway, wonders Destiny? Of course, the answer is clear. Principal Brandfather is envious and wants to stand in the way of Destiny's success.

Well, Destiny isn't going to let that stop her. She'll just go back to one of her old schools and ask them. She shouldn't have any problem. But it does mean more time spent driving and collecting data, something Destiny has very little of.

As Destiny gets into her truck, she realizes she will never let anyone stand in her way. Not ever. And least of all, Principal Brandfather.

Chapter 5
Julie

It's Saturday morning and Calix has taken Georgia to the park. Destiny is home, working on her thesis research, but she can't seem to concentrate. She's been thinking about Katie and wants to share her good news with her.

She decides to try calling Katie again. A recording comes on. "I'm sorry, that number is unavailable," says the tinny voice.

Katie has completely blocked Destiny's number!

Maybe Destiny should just drive over there and speak to Katie face-to-face. However, she decides that might not be the best idea. Instead, she gives Julie a call.

After three rings, Julie picks up. "Hi Julie, it's Destiny."

"Oh, hi, Destiny."

"Listen, I was wondering if you'd like to come over for lunch. We haven't seen each other in a while and I'd really like to get your take on Katie and why she is still avoiding me."

"I don't know," says Julie, hesitantly. "I've got a lot of errands to run today."

"Surely one of them must bring you close to my place."

"Yeah, I guess so. Okay, I'll come. How is 12:30?"

"That sounds great," says Destiny.

"Okay, see you then."

By the time Julie rings the doorbell, Destiny has a plate of sandwiches and a pitcher of lemonade sitting on the dining table. Destiny answers the door, "Hi, Julie. Come on in."

Julie steps in. "Hi, Destiny."

After Julie takes her shoes off, they make their way to the dining room.

"How have you been?" asks Destiny as they sit down.

"I've been fine? You?"

"Great, thanks."

"And Georgia? Is she here? I'd love to see her."

"No, Calix has her out for the afternoon. But I do have some news. We're going to have another baby."

"Wow!" says Julie, taking a bite of her sandwich. "That's great."

"I know, and I tried to call Katie to tell her, but she's completely blocked my number. I don't know what more I can do. I mean, I know she was upset about what I told her about Fred, but you'd think she would have gotten over it by now."

"Well, the truth is Katie broke up with Fred. She caught him with his ex-girlfriend, Annabelle."

"Really? Then why is she still avoiding me?"

"Because she blames you for the breakup."

"She blames me?" Destiny is stunned. "How could that possibly be my fault. I was the one who tried to warn her about Fred. I was trying to save her from getting hurt."

"Listen, Destiny," says Julie. There is hesitation in her voice. "The fact is, you have it so easy. Everything just comes to you. You have the perfect job, the perfect husband, the perfect family. You have your education and your tutoring center. It seems as if nothing can really go wrong for you."

"That's ridiculous. I've had plenty of hardships. My principal is out to get me, for one."

"Yeah, but that's the perfect example. Even though she has it in for you, you're still succeeding. Nothing can stand in your way."

Julie pauses for a moment. "Don't you get it, Destiny? Katie is envious and she feels like you ruined the only thing good in her life. Quite frankly, I'm envious, too. That's why I have always been so distant from you."

Destiny doesn't even know what to say.

"I'm sorry," says Julie, standing up. "I know that's a hard pill to swallow, but..."

"Yeah, well, I didn't realize the people I thought were my friends saw me that way."

"I think I should go. I'm sorry."

Julie goes to the front door, puts on her shoes, and looks back at Destiny, who is following behind her.

"I really am sorry," says Julie.

Then she is gone and Destiny is left wondering where her friendships went so wrong.

Destiny goes through her afternoon in a daze. She can't get her conversation with Julie out of her mind. She tries to call Momma so she can talk to her and get her advice, but

Momma's not home. Then she tries Michelle, but she's not home, either.

That evening at dinner, Destiny picks at her food in silence. Calix is staring at her as Georgia flings peas onto the floor. "What's up?" asks Calix.

"You know I saw Julie today, right?"

Calix nods.

"Well, she said Katie broke up with Fred because she caught him cheating with Annabelle, which is exactly what I warned her would happen. And apparently she blames me for the whole thing."

"That's ridiculous," says Calix.

"That's what I said. Then she told me that Katie is really upset because I have such a perfect life and everything comes so easy for me. And Julie feels the same way. I feel like the friends I once trusted have stabbed me in the back."

"Well, they are jealous of you. You have so much success. But it's not your fault. If they can't handle it or find their own success, that's their problem. They're just blaming you for their own failure because they don't want to face the fact that it's their own responsibility. It's always easier to blame someone else."

"Yeah, I guess so, but I feel like I can't trust my friends anymore. I mean, what if Ethel feels the same way?"

"There's no way she does. She loves you."

Destiny sighs. "Yeah, I guess."

"Listen, I'll clean up and you go get some work done."

"What about Georgia?"

"She can stay here and help me."

Destiny chuckles. "Help you how? By giving you more to clean up?"

"Something like that," says Calix, giving Destiny a hug.

"Thanks," says Destiny, grateful for her husband. She hugs Georgia and heads off to her desk to work. But her evening isn't very productive. Her mind is too distracted, and eventually, she gives up and heads to bed early. Tomorrow will be a better day, she thinks as she drifts off to sleep.

Chapter 6

Data, Envy, and Illness

Destiny looks at her watch as she rushes toward the door of the school. The bell is going to ring in less than 10 minutes. She is cutting it close. But she had to go pick up the data she has been collecting for her PhD thesis. Fortunately, a neighboring school agreed to let her use their students for the study.

As Destiny rushes past the door to the office, Principal Brandfather sees her. Before Destiny can make it to the stairwell, Principal Brandfather calls out her name. Destiny stops in her tracks and turns around.

"Can I see you in my office for a moment?" asks Principal Brandfather.

"Sure," says Destiny, following her through the door and into her office. "But I don't have much time."

"So I noticed. You're in quite a hurry. May I ask where you've been?"

"I have been over at Templeton Middle School, collecting data for my thesis. Since I couldn't collect the data here, I had to make other arrangements."

"I see," says Principal Brandfather. "I have to know, how do you fit everything in, Destiny. You never seem to stop for anything. You are doing your PhD in addition to teaching full-time, being a pregnant mother, and running a tutoring center that is big enough to take on government contracts. Tell me, is your PhD terribly challenging?"

"What do you mean?"

"Well, I just can't see how you can manage it with everything else."

Destiny isn't quite sure what Principal Brandfather is getting at, but she isn't going to bite.

"Well, I guess I thrive on being busy," says Destiny. "And I am trying to keep my career in teaching low-key for now. I am staying away from administrative positions so I have more time to devote to getting my degree."

"I see," says Principal Brandfather.

"I know you have done a lot to get where you are, Daniella, and I respect that. Making the career advancements you have is a true accomplishment, but it has meant you have needed to give yourself to others to make it happen and that has left little time for yourself or for other pursuits. That's just not something I am willing to do right now. Honestly, maybe it's time for you to take a step back and do something for yourself, something you have always wanted to do."

"I see."

The bell rings. "Well, I need to get up to my classroom," says Destiny.

Principal Brandfather nods, but says nothing. As Destiny leaves, she notices a thoughtful look on Principal Brandfather's face.

Destiny runs into Ethel on her way out of her classroom at the end of the day.

"My goodness, Destiny," says Ethel. "You look exhausted. Are you doing okay?"

"I'm fine Ethel, really. I have been more tired and ill with this pregnancy, I'll admit, but I'm sure it will pass soon."

"I hope so, dear. Maybe you should check with your doctor just in case."

"I have a checkup scheduled for next week so I'll ask him then if I still feel this way. But since I have you here, I wanted to ask you something."

"Fire away," says Ethel.

"I had the strangest conversation with Daniella at lunchtime today."

"Oh?"

"She was asking me how I manage everything and I get the impression she was implying my degree is not reputable. She didn't say that in so many words, but... Anyway, I told her I chose to pursue my degree instead of pursuing an administrative position and that maybe she should consider stepping back and deciding to do something for herself."

"What did she say?"

"Nothing, but she had a look on her face, like she was thinking about something."

"You know she's working on her PhD, right?"

"No, I didn't!"

"She's been working on it for years. And here you come, young and committed and balancing so many things. You make it look so easy and I think she's jealous that you are accomplishing so much at your age."

"Juggling everything I have going on is anything but easy," says Destiny. "But really, we all make choices. I'm not responsible for it if she didn't make the right ones."

"I know, dear. But she can't see that. Instead, she tries to find ways to justify your success. I've heard her talking you know, in the staff room when you're not around."

"About what?"

"About how you must be cheating somehow with your degree. Either that or the degree is really low-quality and not worth the paper it's written on."

"That's ridiculous!"

"Listen, I know, but that's how she feels. But who knows, maybe you have given her something new to think about."

"Yeah, maybe."

"Now, go home and get some rest."

"I will. Thanks, Ethel.

That evening, Destiny can't even bring herself to cook dinner. She feels nauseous and exhausted. She gives Georgia something to eat and decides Calix will have to fend for himself.

"That's fine," Calix says when he gets home. "You just go rest."

"I have work to do," says Destiny. "I have a ton of data to organize."

"Well, don't be at it too long," he says. "You don't look so good."

"I don't feel so good, either."

Destiny tries to get through the data she has collected. She gets a start on charting it properly, but her stomach is so upset she can't keep at it for long. She ends up going to bed shortly after 7:00 pm. Calix takes care of Georgia.

Part 3:
Trust Issues

Chapter 7
Bed Rest

"Well, Destiny," says Dr. Henderson, "looking at your bloodwork, you are slightly anemic, but I think that's only part of the problem. I believe you are simply under too much stress."

"I guess so," says Destiny. "I'm very busy, that's for sure. But I was able to handle things when I was pregnant with Georgia."

"What's changed?"

"Nothing, really."

"What's the most stressful thing in your life right now? What could be triggering this?"

"Honestly, that would be my principal. She has made my life at the school very difficult."

"I see. Well, I'm ordering bed rest for the remainder of your pregnancy."

"Bed rest? But I can't do that. I have too much to do. There must be another way."

"Destiny, your first priority is to take care of yourself and the baby. Nothing is more important than that. Now, you can still work on your PhD thesis at home, but I want you to slow down. And I especially want you to take time away from the school. Your principal isn't doing you any good at all."

"I know you're right, but I don't know how easy it will be to get the time off. She certainly won't be happy about it."

"Why don't you let me worry about that? On your way out, Christine will give you a letter that you can take to the school. No one will question it and you shouldn't have any trouble at all."

"Okay, thanks," says Destiny.

Dr. Henderson leaves the room and Destiny follows shortly behind. She feels miserable. How can she stop working? How can she leave her students? She knows it's the right thing to do for the baby, but that doesn't make it any easier.

She waits a few minutes for the letter from Dr. Henderson and then heads home.

When Calix gets home that evening, Destiny has a simple supper on the table. She's so exhausted it's all she can do. She is sitting at the table, her cheeks showing dried up trails that betray the tears she has shed.

Calix looks concerned. "What's wrong? Is everything okay with the baby?"

"Yes, the baby's fine. But Dr. Henderson says I have to stop working and be on bed rest for the rest of my pregnancy. He says the stress of the school environment is not good for me and I need to slow down." Tears start streaming down her face once again as she says this.

"Is that all?"

"What do you mean, is that all?" sniffs Destiny.

"I just meant you and the baby are safe. That's all that really matters."

"I just don't know how I'll manage. I have so much going on, so much to do."

Calix hugs her. "Maybe this is just what you needed to make you slow down. Everything will be just fine, Destiny. You'll see."

"I guess so," Destiny replies, but Calix doesn't sound nearly as sympathetic as she expected he would. There is almost a lightness to his voice, like he's happy with the situation. Relieved, even.

The doorbell rings before Destiny gets a chance to ask Calix about it. "That's Madeline," says Calix. "I'll take Georgia and get her some dinner."

They open the door. As Calix takes Georgia from Madeline, he says, "She was good today?"

"She's been an absolute angle, as always," says Madeline.

Destiny gives Georgia a kiss before Calix whisks her away. Madeline looks at Destiny and says, "What's wrong, honey? You look upset."

"My doctor told me I need bed rest for the rest of the pregnancy. I have to stop teaching for the rest of the year."

"Well, it's about time someone made you slow down. You have been running yourself ragged and that baby in there is more important than teaching or degrees or anything else."

"I know, but..."

"There are no buts. You listen to your doctor and I am here. I will help out in any way I can."

"I know you will and thank you so much."

"Now, you get in there and enjoy your family. That's what it's all about right now."

The next morning, Destiny is waiting for Principal Brandfather as she arrives.

"You're here early," says Principal Brandfather.

"I know," says Destiny. "I need to speak with you."

"Alright, come on in," Principal Brandfather says as she unlocks her office door.

She drops her keys on her desk and asks, "What do you need?"

Destiny holds out the letter the doctor gave her to give to the school and says, "My doctor has told me I need to be on bed rest for the rest of my pregnancy. I have to stop teaching for the rest of the year."

"What?" Principal Brandfather opens the letter and reads it. Then she sighs. "Well, now what are we going to do?"

"Sorry," says Destiny.

"What will we do without you? I'm going to have to find a replacement. You can't stay today?"

Destiny shakes her head.

"Alright. I'll need to get on the phone and get someone in here."

"Thank you, Daniella."

"Well, it's not like I have much choice. But I guess, if you need to take care of your baby, well, there it is." Principal Brandfather sits down at her desk and picks up the phone.

"Okay, well I'll go clear out of my classroom."

Principal Brandfather nods as she stars dialing a number.

Wow, she didn't even ask if I was okay or show any genuine concern at all, Destiny thinks as she walks out of the office and up to her classroom. Destiny doesn't understand how someone can be that cold.

Once upstairs, Destiny clears a few of her personal belongings out of her desk. Then she writes a note to her students, apologizing that she won't be able to finish the year with them and wishing them the best of luck. She leaves the note on the desk for the replacement teacher to see.

In the hallway, she sees Ethel. "What are you doing with that bag of stuff?" asks Ethel. "You look like you're moving out."

"I am."

"What? What's happened?"

"My doctor told me I have to take the rest of the year off. I've been under too much stress, particularly around here."

"Well, I can vouch for that," says Ethel. "And I'm glad someone's making you slow down."

Destiny laughs. "That's exactly what Madeline said when I told her."

"You just take care of yourself and that baby. Everything here will be just fine."

"I know," says Destiny. "And I will."

"And give Georgia a big kiss for Aunty Ethel," Ethel says as she gives Destiny a big hug. "We'll miss you around here."

"I'll be back," says Destiny.

"Oh, I know you will."

They say their goodbyes and Destiny heads home. At least I can keep myself busy with my thesis work, Destiny thinks. Plus, I'll have some quality time with Georgia before the baby's born. She is trying to look at the situation in the most positive light. It's hard, but what choice does she have?

Chapter 8
Calix Lies

Destiny is sitting on the sofa with her feet stretched out in front of her and her laptop open. But she isn't looking at her screen. Instead, she is staring out the window at the gorgeous day.

Destiny has been home now for nearly a month. And she's bored. It's not that she doesn't have anything to do, but just being home all the time and sitting around so much is really getting to her.

Georgia is at Madeline's house, as she is every morning. And being home alone so much, Destiny has learned to appreciate the expression "the silence is deafening." The street is quiet through the day. There aren't a lot of people around, except the odd mother taking her child to the park.

It's probably not totally quiet, but Destiny is used to the buzz of the classroom all day. Compared to that, she feels like she's in a soundproof booth.

Destiny decides she needs to get up and move around. The doctor told her she should get some light exercise, such as walking, every day. Now seems like a good time to go. Madeline is bringing Georgia home after lunch.

Destiny steps out into the sun and decides she will walk past the park, which is a couple of blocks down the street. The sound of the children playing in the park soothes her. It feels good to hear them. She misses her class, but she knows this time off is for the best. Besides, she is getting some extra special time with Georgia before the baby is born.

As she stands and watches the children in the park, Destiny rests her hand on her belly, which is just starting to show her pregnancy. She smiles as she thinks of the new addition to her family. It might not have been planned, but she certainly welcomes this new life.

The only real downside right now, other than being cooped up, is that Calix has been so busy with work. He's never been this busy before, but his company picked up a government construction contract and he has been working a lot of extra hours. She knows it's a good thing, but she hardly sees him these days and she misses him.

At least the construction season will be wrapping up around the time the baby is born. Then they can enjoy the summer together as a family of four.

Destiny gets home just as Madeline is bringing Georgia down the street. Georgia sees her and starts running. Then she falls and scrapes her knee.

"Oh darling, let me see," says Destiny, bending down.

"That child is getting faster every day," says Madeline.

"I know it," says Destiny. "Thanks for keeping her this morning. I managed to get a lot done and even went for a walk."

"That's good to hear. Calix gonna be home this evening?"

Destiny shakes her head as she picks up Georgia. "No, he has to work late again. And he has to work all weekend. Apparently, they need him on another job site, somewhere north of here."

"Well, I guess that means more money. Can't have too much of that, now can we?"

"That's true."

Madeline kisses Georgia. "See you tomorrow morning, sweetie. And you take care of yourself," she says to Destiny.

"I will."

That afternoon, after Destiny has had some playtime with Georgia and settled her down for a nap, she is once again sitting on the sofa. As she reads a paper, she hears a phone ringing from the other side of the room.

She gets up and goes over. It's Calix's phone sitting on the table by the armchair. He must have forgotten to take it with him today. Destiny looks at the number on the phone, but doesn't recognize it.

She picks it up to answer it, but before she can say a word, a woman on the other end of the line says, "Hey, baby! We all set for our trip this weekend?"

"Excuse me?" says Destiny.

"Who is this?" asks the woman.

That's precisely what Destiny wants to know, but something tells her to tread carefully. "This is Jennifer, Calix's sister. Who may I ask is calling?"

"This is Liz, Calix's girlfriend. I want to make sure our weekend away is still on. Can you pass on the message for me?"

Destiny feels a bit dizzy as she answers, "Yeah, sure."

"Thanks, doll," says Liz. Then she's gone, and for a moment, Destiny just stands there with Calix's phone to her ear. Then the fury and hurt begin to take the place of shock and she heads upstairs. She has a solution to this problem.

An hour later, between tears and getting Georgia up from her nap, Destiny has a bag packed for Calix. She's exhausted, partly from the physical effort and partly from the emotional strain.

The evening passes. Georgia eats dinner and Destiny puts her to bed. Destiny doesn't feel like eating much. When Calix gets home, it's dark out. Destiny is standing in the front hallway waiting for him, with his phone in her hand and his bag at her feet.

When he comes in the door, he looks confused. "What's all this about. I don't leave for the other job site until Thursday."

"Really?" says Destiny. "The other job site?" She waves his phone in the air. "I took a call for you today. Your girlfriend, Liz, wants to know if your weekend away is still a go. I'd like to know that, too, Calix. Is your weekend away with your girlfriend still a go?"

For a moment, Calix is silent. "Destiny, I can explain..."

"You mean you can tell me more lies and excuses."

"No, really, I..."

"There never was any overtime, was there? How long has this been going on? Since before I got pregnant? No, never mind. I don't want to know. I just want you out of here."

"Come on, Destiny. Please, let's talk about this."

"There is nothing to talk about. You have a girlfriend so go talk to her."

"Destiny, please..."

"Get out!"

Calix looks at her for a moment and then he steps forward and picks up his bag. Destiny passes him his phone, turns, and walks upstairs. She hears the door shut a minute later.

That night, Destiny cries herself to sleep.

Chapter 9

The Visit

"N ow, don't you worry about a thing," says Madeline. "Georgia is fine. You just go show that new baby off to everyone at work." Madeline is right about Georgia, who is already sitting at her little table in the living room, coloring in her princess coloring book.

"I will," says Destiny. "Thanks so much for doing this on such short notice."

"Don't you know by now, honey, that I'm at your beck and call? Well, actually, I'm at these children's beck and call. I can't resist them for anything!"

Destiny laughs. "I know it."

Destiny leaves Madeline's house and walks down the sidewalk carrying Amaiya Linelle in her car seat. Amaiya was born a month early, but she was healthy. What a gift.

Now, Destiny is happy to be off bedrest and able to get back to a regular routine. And even though Destiny is often up in the night, Amaiya generally sleeps well and Destiny is feeling much stronger than before the baby was born.

Calix's dishonesty was a blow at a time that was already difficult for Destiny. Since Amaiya was born, he has been visiting the children, but that's as far as Destiny will let it go. He wants to reconcile, to be given another chance, but Destiny will have none of it.

Just this morning, he said, "Just think of the happy family we can be if we can just work this out."

Destiny's reply was short. "There is nothing to work out, Calix. I deserve better than what you have to offer."

He seemed devastated, but he didn't say another word about it. Instead he focused on his daughters.

As Destiny clips Amaiya's car seat into its base and closes the truck door, she smiles to herself. Yes, she feels strong. Even strong enough to face Principal Brandfather after all this time.

When Destiny walks into the school office, Sheree is up out of her seat before Destiny can say a word.

"Let me see that beautiful baby," says Sheree. Amaiya is just waking up and Sheree is undoing the straps of the car seat before Destiny has the chance to set it down.

In no time, Sheree is walking around the office cooing and murmuring to Amaiya.

"I'm here, too," says Destiny. "In case you didn't notice."

"Oh, sugar, I know it. But I need to see this little child. I'll see plenty of you soon enough. And look at this outfit! It's darling!"

The outfit is a little pink and white onesie with a hood and hand covers that make Amaiya look like a teddy bear. "Momma sent that. She can't stop buying baby clothes, even though I still have everything Goergia wore."

"She's a grandmama. You are not going to get her to stop. You know that, right?"

"Yeah, I know," says Destiny.

"Now, tell me how you're feeling?"

Destiny's friends were a rock for her when she kicked Calix out. They all made sure she got through the pregnancy while on bed rest and on her own.

"I'm just fine," says Destiny. "Better than ever, actually."

"And that *man*?" That is all Sheree will call Calix. She never uses his name anymore.

"He tried again this morning and I simply told him I deserve better."

"That's right, honey. And speaking of better, did you hear about Daniella?"

"No, what's up?" Destiny silently wonders if Principal Brandfather has found someone new to target since she has been on leave.

"Apparently, she's going on a leave of absence."

"Really? Why?"

Sheree shrugs as she cradles Amaiya. "No idea. She hasn't told anyone, at least not yet."

"Huh," says Destiny. She thinks she might know why Principal Brandfather is taking leave, but it isn't her place to say.

"You know something I don't?" asks Sheree.

"No. Just surprised, that's all. She in?"

"Not right now, but maybe you can catch her later."

"Alright, well I had better take Amaiya and make the rounds. I'll be back in a little while."

Sheree reluctantly hands Amaiya over and Destiny sets off for the second floor in search of Edith.

✧ ✧ ✧

It's nearly two hours later when Destiny returns to the office with a sleeping Amaiya in her arms. She lays Amaiya in her car seat and she doesn't even stir.

"That is one tired baby," says Sheree.

"That's what happens when you get passed around a school for two hours. I'm tired, too."

Destiny can hear Principal Brandfather in her office, so she takes Amaiya, car seat and all, and knocks on Principal Brandfather's office door.

"Oh, Destiny. Come on in," says Principal Brandfather.

"I hope I'm not interrupting."

"Not at all."

"I just thought you might want to meet Amaiya," says Destiny, setting the car seat on the table in the corner of the office. "It seems that you get the sleepy baby, rather than the awake baby, I'm afraid."

Principal Brandfather comes over and looks at Amaiya. "She is absolutely beautiful. And they are so peaceful when they're sleeping."

"Yes, they are."

They stand watching Amaiya for a moment, then Destiny says, "I hear you're going on leave."

Principal Brandfather nods. "Yes, Destiny, you have inspired me. Thanks to the advice you gave me, I have decided to take some time off to finish my PhD."

"Really? That's wonderful!"

Principal Brandfather looks at Destiny. "Listen, I know I haven't always been easy to work for."

Destiny doesn't know what to say, but the expression on her face gives her away.

"I know, I've been hard on you. And I'm sorry for that. I am so happy that you have been patient and stuck with me. With the school."

"I... Well, thank you."

The next thing Destiny knows, Principal Brandfather is giving her a hug. "You take care of those children and yourself, Destiny. You truly are an inspiration, and not just for the students you teach. Even for old folks like me."

Destiny is touched and more than a little shocked. She says her goodbyes to Principal Brandfather and wishes her luck with her PhD. Then she takes Amaiya out into the main office.

Sheree looks at her and mouths, "What happened?"

Destiny just raises her eyebrows and smiles. She can't believe what just happened. But she is so pleased about it she can't help grinning as she heads out to her truck.

REVELATIONS

Chapter 10
Epilogue

The drive home that day is quiet. It's still early afternoon so traffic is light. Amaiya is sleeping, and as she drives, Destiny's mind wanders to Principal Brandfather.

She is stunned at the difference in Principal Brandfather's attitude with her. That she would give Destiny a hug, let alone greet her with any warmth or friendship, or even as a colleague, is completely unbelievable.

Yet, she did, and Destiny realizes how much of a positive influence she has been on Principal Brandfather. Destiny has always thought that Principal Brandfather was jealous Destiny's success and she still thinks that. But there is more to it than simple jealousy.

Principal Brandfather has attained a level of success that many would be happy with, but she definitely wants more. It's obvious to Destiny that she feels bad that she hasn't achieved the same level of success as Destiny has. And she had been taking her frustrations out on Destiny. Yet, it turns out she really values Destiny's experience and opinion. She just never knew how to express it appropriately.

Destiny thinks about it. If she can have that level of positive impact on Principal Brandfather of all people, then surely, she can have an impact on other people. Maybe, just maybe, Destiny is having a positive impact on the people in her life and doesn't know it, people like Katie and Julie.

Too bad that impact didn't reach Calix, Destiny thinks. But despite his betrayal, Destiny feels strong and confident in her abilities and the direction her life has taken. And she is grateful for that because she is now single-handedly raising two girls and she wants them to grow into successful, confident women.

Since she isn't due home for a little while and Amaiya is sleeping soundly, Destiny decides to take a little time for herself. She pulls into one of her favorite diners. Careful not to wake Amaiya, Destiny carries the car seat inside.

"Hello there," says Debra, the waitress who often serves Destiny when she comes in. "Is this your new little one?"

Destiny nods.

"No wonder I haven't seen you in here in a while. She's beautiful! How old?"

"Three weeks tomorrow," says Destiny.

"Well, what can I get you?"

"I would love a hot cup of tea and a piece of pecan pie."

"Coming right up," says Debra.

Five minutes later, Destiny is savoring her pie, which doesn't last long. She savors the peacefulness of the quiet diner. Life is definitely good, thinks Destiny, as she holds her warm cup in her hands and gazes out the window. It's at that moment that Amaiya stirs and begins to fuss. Destiny chuckles to herself. Life *is* good.

www.ingramcontent.com/pod-product-compliance
Lightning Source LLC
Chambersburg PA
CBHW071208130626
46555CB00004B/1630